ANTONIO GHISLANZONI (1824-1893) was an Italian opera singer and man of letters. Though primarily remembered today for writing the libretto for Verdi's *Aida*, he wrote a vast number of other works, including around eighty librettos, numerous lyrics, at least seven novels, a large number of short stories, and hundreds of newspaper articles. Closely associated with the Scapigliatura movement, many of his items of fiction, such as his 1884 novel *Abrakadabra*, have elements of the fantastic.

BRENDAN and ANNA CONNELL have together translated numerous texts from Italian, including *Alcina and Other Stories* (Snuggly Books, 2019) by Guido Gozzano, Ruggero Vasari's Futurist play *Raun* (Snuggly Books, 2023), and *Narcisa and Other Stories* (Snuggly Books, 2024), by Luigi Gualdo.

SNUGGLY BOOKS

ANTONIO GHISLANZONI

THE VIOLIN WITH HUMAN STRINGS
AND OTHER TALES
OF MUSICAL MADNESS

TRANSLATED BY
BRENDAN AND ANNA CONNELL

THIS IS A SNUGGLY BOOK

ISBN: 978-1-64525-163-7

Contents

Introduction

ANTONIO GHISLANZONI (1824-1893) was born in Lecco and, due to the desires of his father, studied in the Seminario di Castello, before being expelled at the age of seventeen for irreverent behavior. He was transferred to Pavia, where he finished high school and then, in 1843, enrolled in the faculty of medicine. His true interest, however, was not medicine, but music, and, quitting Pavia, he moved to Lovere, where he studied singing at the Istituto di belle arti Tadini (currently the Accademia Tadini). Having mastered his art, he signed a five-year contract with an impresario in Milan and made his debut in Lodi as a baritone and subsequently appeared, with much praise, at the Teatro Carcano in Milan.

His talents, however, were not confined to music, and he had begun to place reviews, poems and stories in various newspapers; and then, prompted by the Revolutions of 1848, he founded his own paper *Il Repubblicano*, and for a brief period in the same year edited a daily, the *Dialogo del Popolo*.

In 1849 he was arrested by the French and locked in the Bastia in Rome. Two years later he was performing Verdi's *Ernani* at the Théâtre des Italiens in Paris, and three years after that, in 1855, his last singing performance took place in Milan—and it was at this point that he made letters as his sole profession.

In 1857 he began to serialize a novel called *Gli artisti da Teatro* [The Artists of the Theatre], based on his experiences, and the same year wrote his first libretto, *Le due fidanzate*, for the young composer Antonio Baur (1830-1874). This was followed in 1858 by the libretto *Il Conte di Leicester*, also for Baur, commissioned by the Teatro Regio in Parma.

Ghislanzoni was writing furiously. In 1857 his novel *Le memorie di un gatto* [Memoirs of a Cat] appeared; in 1859 he published around 150 articles in *Cosmorama pittorico,* and in the following years had regular columns in numerous journals, including *Lombardia*, *La Settimana illustrata*, *L'Alleanza*, and *L'Illustrazione sociale*. Furthermore, through his work on the *Rivista minima*, his name became associated with the Scapigliatura movement; and though he himself was not necessarily fond of the label, his own work was quite influential, his *Le donne brutte* [The Ugly Women] (1867) providing inspiration for the novels of I.U. Tarchetti.

As a librettist, Ghislanzoni's fame had become great; and when the Khedivial Opera House in Cairo commission an opera from Verdi, it was Ghislanzoni whom he selected to write the libretto, the masterpiece *Aida* debuting in 1871.

The opera was a huge success, and today Ghislanzoni is primarily remembered for its libretto. Unfortunately, in the contract for his composition, he opted for a one-time payment rather than accepting royalties, which would have allowed him a more stress-free existence, instead of the constant demands of production with which he was engaged in throughout his life.

L'arte di far debiti (1881), *La contessa di Karolystria* (1883), and his fantastic novel *Abrakadabra* (1884)—these were just some of the books the vocalist turned man-of-letters completed in his mature years before, in 1890, starting a newspaper, *La Posta di Caprino* which he wrote almost entirely himself.

Though little known outside of Italy, and also mostly forgotten in Italy, Antonio Ghislanzoni was indubitably one of the most important Italian writers of his time. In all, he wrote around eighty librettos, numerous lyrics, at least seven novels, a large number of short stories, and hundreds of newspaper articles.

※

Ghislanzoni's wide experience in the world of music certainly informed the short stories in the present collection, all of which were taken from *Racconti e novelle* (1874). Three of these, "Daniel Nabaäm De-Schudmoëken," "Rubly's Trumpet," and "Autobiography of an Ex-Vocalist," were previously translated, rather loosely, and somewhat incompletely, in the *Magazine of Music* in the late 1880s, by Harold Oakley, though never compiled into a book. These documents, naturally, were consulted in making the present translations.

Though "The Violin with Human Strings" appears here in English translation for the first time, it should be noted that another version of the story did previously appear in English under the title "The Ensouled Violin," being a plagiarism by the famous mystic Madame Blavatsky (1831-1891) which was published in the January 1880 issue of *The Theosophist*, under the byline Hillarion Smerdis (one of her supposed masters). She published a longer version of the story later, in her 1892 collection *Nightmare Tales*, in which she went to considerable pains to change many of the details, very likely to make it less traceable to its original source.

—Brendan Connell

THE VIOLIN WITH HUMAN STRINGS

AND OTHER TALES OF MUSICAL MADNESS

The Violin with Human Strings

IT was the year 1831.

The diabolical Paganini[1] had played six concerts at the Opera, stirring up even greater enthusiasm than that which had accompanied him during his triumphal excursions in Italy and Germany.—In the presence of that phenomenal artist, some members of the orchestra of the great theatre had broken their instruments.

---

1 Niccolò Paganini, 1782-1840, Italian composer and the most famous violin virtuoso of his time. When he played gentle pieces, his audience frequently burst into tears; but he was best known for his technical wizardry and the ease and velocity with which he would perform difficult pieces. His dark hair and pale sunken face gave him a "diabolical" appearance.

During the same period there was in Paris another violinist, gifted with extraordinary ability, but still ignored by the great world of art. His name was Franz Sthoeny. He was born in Stockard, and in that city had spent his youth in the peace of the family, alternating severe philosophic meditations with exercises on the four-stringed instrument.

At the age of thirty-five, Franz had been left an orphan and alone. Upon the death of his mother, who had adored him, who for her only child had exhausted all the savings of an extremely feeble patrimony, Franz realised that he was poor.

His future prospects appeared to him in the most dismal colours.

What to do? His old music teacher Samuele Klauss had charged himself with the task of answering that terrible question. And the reply, without words, had been eloquent.

Klauss had taken his beloved student by the hand and, having led him to the small room where many times they had shared together the fantastic joys of music, had pointed out to him the small case where the violin lay shut like a living being in a forgotten tomb.

That gesture opened up a new career for Franz Sthoeny. After selling his furniture and other household articles, the artist left for Paris in the company of his teacher and friend.

Before Paganini gave his marvellous concerts at the theatre of the Opera, Franz, due to a series of experiences and comparisons, had a superb conviction and an immovable resolution. His conviction was this: that he considered himself superior to all the most renowned violinists he had heard in the capital of France,—his resolution was to break his own instrument, and his existence with it, if he did not succeed in holding the first place among the players of the age. Old Klauss took pleasure in this noble pride and believed, in good faith, that by flattering him he was performing a saintly deed.

But before giving a public appearance Franz waited with trembling impatience for the much praised Italian to have his debut in Paris. The name of Paganini had been, for some months, a red-hot thorn in the heart of

Franz—a nightmare, a menacing phantom to the spirit of old Samuel.

Each had trembled more than once at that artist's name—as each had ominously foretold his coming to Paris.

Who can describe the anxieties, the spasms and the atrocious enthusiasm of that ill-fated evening?—Franz and Samuel, at the first arc of Paganini's bow, shuddered. The teacher and the pupil, stricken by an enthusiasm which was a tremendous distress to them both, did not dare to look each other in the face, or exchange a word.

At midnight, after the concert, they returned mute and gloomy to their apartment.

"Samuele!" Franz said, casting himself upon a chair in a desperate manner. "You see! . . . the two of us are good for nothing—understand?—for nothing! . . . really for nothing! . . ."

The old teacher's wrinkled skin turned livid.—After a brief silence Samuele replied in a sullen voice:

"But you are wrong Franz—I have taught you as much as a teacher can teach, and you have learned everything one man can learn from another. Is it my fault if these damned Italians, in order to excel in the realm of art, have resorted to the inspirations of the devil and to the shames of magic?"[1]

Franz, with a sinister expression, fixed his eyes on those of the old teacher:—and his gaze seemed to say: "Very well then! why so many scruples? . . . If I too could be elevated to such artistic power, I would also give myself to the devil, body and soul!"

Samuele divined that atrocious thought and, with feigned calm, continued to speak:

"You know the miserable story of the celebrated Tartini.[2] He died one Saturday night, strangled by his familiar demon, who had taught him how to give a soul to a violin by incorporating in it the spirit of a virgin. Paganini has done more. Paganini, in order to commu-

---

1 It was commonly believed that Paganini had entered on a pact with the devil. On one occasion, in Vienna, a member of the audience became crazed and declared that he had seen the devil assisting the violinist.

2 Giuseppe Tartini, 1692-1770, Italian violinist and composer. One of his more famous compositions is *The Devil's Sonata*.

nicate to his own instrument the moans, the desolate cries, the most heart-breaking notes of the human voice, became the murderer of the man who cared for him more than anyone on earth, and with the entrails of his victim made the four strings of his enchanted violin. There you have the secret of that fascination, of that irresistible power of sound which you, my dear Franz, would never be able to equal, if first . . ."

And the old man stopped short in the middle the sentence.

His voice was paralysed by a mysterious dismay.

Franz, lowering his eyes, after a few minutes came out with this question:

"And you believe, Samuele, that I too would be able to obtain those unheard of results, to stir up enthusiasm like Paganini, if the strings of my instrument were made of human fibre?"

"Unfortunately!" exclaimed the teacher, with a singular expression. "But in order to obtain such an outcome, it is not enough for the strings simply to be made of human fibre; it is also necessary for this fibre to have been part of a sympathetic person's body. Tartini communicated life to his own violin by introducing into it the soul of a virgin—but the virgin had died of love for him; and that satanic artist, while attending to her during her final agony, made the spirit of the dying girl pass into his instrument with the aid of a straw. As for Paganini, I have already told you that he killed his best friend, the person most bound to him in benevolence—and he killed him in order to tear out his entrails and convert them into so many musical strings.

"Oh! the human voice!—the miracle of human voice," continued Samuele after a brief silence. "Do you believe then, my poor Franz, that I would not have taught you how to produce it, if it was possible to do so through the means of art, through that noble and sacred art which wants to live of itself, which wants to shine with its own light, which disdains meanness and swindle, which is horrified by crimes?"

Franz did not have the strength to utter a word. He stood up with a sinister calmness which revealed the most profound agitation,—he took the violin in his hands,—he fixed a scornful and menacing look on the strings—and then, having seized them with a convulsive impetus, he ripped them from the instrument.

Old Samuele let out a cry. The strings, reduced to a ball, had been cast onto the embers in the fireplace, and there they were writhing and hissing like a group of hibernating snakes at contact with fire.

Samuele removed a candlestick from the table and went to his bedroom without saying goodnight to his friend.

Weeks went by—months went by. A deep melancholy took possession of Franz. The violin, widowed of its strings, hung upon the wall, dusty and neglected. Samuele and Franz had lunch together every day and every evening they sat, one in front of the other, in the same small drawing-room—but each one did not dare to address a word to the other, so they looked at each other in silence, like two mutes. —From the moment the violin was without strings, those two living beings seemed also to have lost the power of speech.

"It is time for all this to end!" old Samuele finally exclaimed. And that night, before retiring to his bedroom, he drew nearer to his friend to imprint a kiss on his forehead. Franz roused himself from his sad lethargy, and repeated mechanically the words of his teacher: "It is time for all this to end!"

They parted—and each went to bed.

The next morning, when Franz opened his eyes to the light of day, he was surprised not to find next to his bed the old teacher who usually awoke before him.

"Samuele! My good . . . my excellent Samuele!" Franz cried, jumping out of the blankets and rushing into the room of his teacher.

Franz was terrified by his own voice but even more so by the lugubrious silence which answered it.

There are deep silences which announce death.

Near the beds of the deceased and the openings of tombs silence acquires a mysterious intensity which strikes terror into the soul.

The severe head of Samuele lay stiff against the bolster—the salient outlines of that head were a bald brow blazing with light and a pointed grey beard which seemed to raise itself to the heavens.

Franz experienced a terrible shock upon seeing the cadaver—but human nature and the nature of the artist both awoke in him at the same time, and in that struggle of sentiments grief was soon left paralysed. The passion of the artist prevailed over the most tender instincts of the man and suffocated them.

A letter addressed to Franz lay on the night-table. The violinist opened it, trembling.

> My dear Franz,
>
> By the time you read this writing I will have accomplished the greatest and last sacrifice that I, your teacher and only friend, could for your glory. The person who loved you more than anyone else in the world is now nothing more than an unfeeling body. Today, in front of you, there

remains of your old teacher nothing but impassive organic matter. I will not suggest what is left for you to do.

Do not let vain scruples or foolish superstitions terrorise you. I immolate my corpse to you so that you can use it for your own glory—you would stain yourself with the blackest ingratitude if you made my sacrifice useless. When you have given strings back to your violin—when these strings have been made of my fibre and have the voice, the moan, the cry of my fervid love—then, oh Franz, do not fear anybody—then take your instrument, put yourself on the track of the man who has done us so much harm—present yourself in the field where he has been allowed to rule until this day—cast in his face the glove of challenge! Oh! You will hear how the note of love will issue forcefully from your violin, when caressing the strings you will remember that they were part of your old teacher who now kisses you for the last time and blesses you.

SAMUELE

Two tears sprang from Franz's eyes, but they soon seemed to dry up under the effect of a latent blush. The eyes of the extraordinary musician, fixed on the dead man, flashed like those of an owl.

Our pen shrinks from describing what occurred in that death-chamber after the doctors had made an autopsy of the cadaver. It is enough for us to mention that the last wish of the heroic Samuele was fulfilled and that Franz did not hesitate for a moment to gain possession of the fatal strings with which he hoped to give a soul to his violin.

Those strings, within fifteen days, were stretched on the instrument. Franz did not dare to look at them. One evening he wanted to attempt to play, but the bow trembled in his hand like the blade of a rapier in the fist of a debutant assassin.

"It doesn't matter!" Franz exclaimed, putting the violin back in its case. "These foolish terrors shall disappear once I find myself in the presence of my powerful rival. The last wish of my poor Samuele shall be accomplished . . . and it shall be a great triumph for us both . . . if I am able to equal . . . to excel Paganini!"

But the celebrated violinist was no longer in Paris. At the time Paganini was giving a series of concerts at the theatre of Gand.

One evening, while the diabolical artist was sitting at table surrounded by an elect company of musicians, Franz came into the room of the hotel and, approaching Paganini, without uttering a word, handed him his visiting card.

Paganini read—and then cast on the stranger one of those fulminous looks that even the bravest of men cannot withstand. But seeing that the other remained firm and at the same time seemed to challenge him with the impassibility of his own gaze, he said sharply:

"Sir, your wish will be granted!"—And Franz, after courteously bowing to the guests, left the room.

Two days later a notice was displayed in the city of Gand announcing the last concert of Paganini. On the last lines of the programme, printed in very large letters, stood a peculiar note which excited the public's curiosity to the highest pitch and which was the object of a thousand comments!

On this same evening the note said *the distinguished German violinist Mr. Franz Sthoeny will appear for the first time, having arrived in Gand expressly for the purpose of issuing a challenge to the illustrious Paganini, declaring himself ready to compete with him in the execution of the most difficult pieces. As the illustrious Paganini has accepted the challenge, Mr. Franz Sthoeny must perform, matched against that unsurpassed violinist, the famous* FANTASIA-CAPRICCIO *entitled* THE WITCHES.

The effect of that announcement was magnetic. Paganini, who even in the midst of excitement and triumphs, never lost sight of the bright spot of speculation, thought it proper for that occasion to double the price of the tickets.—It is unnecessary to say that he had calculated perfectly. That evening the whole city of Gand seemed to pour into the theatre.

At the terrible hour of the competition, Franz took himself to the greenroom, where Paganini had preceded him.

"Good fellow!" Paganini said, "you did well to arrive early. It would be good for us to reverse the order of the programme. I am anxious to settle this matter so as not to be disturbed during the execution of my other pieces.—Are you ready?"

"I am at your disposal," Franz calmly replied.

Paganini ordered the curtains to be raised and at once presented himself on the stage amidst a hurricane of applause and frenetic cheers.

Never before had the Italian artist, while playing that diabolical composition entitled *The Witches*, revealed such diabolical power. The strings of the violin, beneath the pressure of his lean fingers, contorted themselves like palpitating entrails—the satanic eyes of the violinist evoked hell from the mysterious cavities of his instrument.—The sounds took on form and it seemed as if, around that musical wizard, fantastical figures obscenely danced. On the emptiness of the stage an inexplicable phantasmagoria formed by the resonant vibrations represented the impudent orgies and the obscure unions of a witch's Sabbath.

When Paganini was finally able to retire from the scene, where at each moment he had been recalled by the uproarious applause of the public, he went to the greenroom and encountered Franz, who had just finished tuning his own violin and was now ready to throw himself into the tournament.

Paganini was amazed at the impassibility of his competitor, and the air of certainty which shone on his face.

Franz advanced onto the stage, greeted by a glacial silence. Subjugated by Paganini's charm, the audience looked at the new-comer as one would some poor simpleton who is facing an absurd test.

Nevertheless, at the first arcs of Franz's bow, the attention of the audience became acute.

Franz was an extremely skilful performer, one of those performers for whom difficulties do not exist. Old Samuele had not lied the day when he told him: I have taught you everything that can be taught, and you have learned everything that can be learned.

But that which Franz had dreamt of obtaining from the effect of the sympathetic strings—the wail of passion, the torturing cry of agony, the roar of the forest and the howl of the damned—that which Samuele would have liked to communicate to his student and friend, by sacrificing himself and endowing this instrument with human strings, this whole edifice of illusions and hopes, which in the soul of the German artist had turned into firm faith—everything vanished in a second . . .

Under the blow of a terrible disillusion, Franz lost courage and strength. . . . Very softly he invoked the name of his teacher—he begged him . . . he secretly cursed him in his soul—and decried him as a wicked traitor. Then, tired out by the trial, made desperate by the denouement, he tore the fatal strings from the violin, flung them on the floor, and trampled on them in ferocious rage.

"He's mad! He's mad!—stop him . . . help him!" a hundred voices shouted from the stalls.

Franz left the stage and, hastily entering the wings, went to prostrate himself at the feet of Paganini.

"Forgive me! A thousand times, forgive me!" Franz cried desperately. "I had believed . . . I had hoped . . ."

Paganini offered a hand to that poor defeated man and, raising him up, embracing him as a brother, said to him:

"You have played divinely . . . you are a great artist . . . what you are missing is . . ."

"Oh! I know very well what I am missing," Franz exclaimed sobbing, "but old Samuele has betrayed me! . . ."

And Franz narrated to Paganini the story of the human strings, ingenuously exposing the illusions he had believed in.

"Poor Franz!" exclaimed the Italian violinist with sarcastic pity, "you have forgotten a certain detail in which the strings of your violin could not compete with mine in vivacity, warmth, the impetus of passion . . . Have you not said that your old teacher was German?"

"Without a doubt—he was as German as I am . . ."

"Well then, it is precisely that detail which is unfavourable," Paganini continued, patting poor Franz on the back. "Next time you want to communicate to your violin the soul, the fire, the passion, the vivacity which I possess, make sure that your strings be made of Italian fibre."

And he added in a whisper, "Also, try to procure for yourself, if you can, the soul of an Italian."[1]

---

1 Paganini actually did have a "duel" with another famous violinist of the time named Lafont, a Frenchman, and won by adding numerous improvisatory octaves, thirds and sixths; but many in the audience believed that he had had supernatural guidance.

Daniel Nabaäm De-Schudmoëken

AT that time, which in many respects resembles the present, I was seated one morning with a few other visitors in the drawing-room of an amiable countess, much celebrated in Milan for her talent as a pianist, and no less so for her beauty and many extravagances.

As usual, we were talking about music; and a discussion was taking place about the supremacy of the German masters, specifically regarding instrumental compositions. The Countess, although extremely Italian in the political sense, professed herself to be German when it came to art.

The conversation was interrupted by a house servant, who, presenting a visiting-card to the Countess, announced the arrival of a new personage.

"Show him in," said the Countess, beaming with pleasure.—And the expression on her face seemed to denote the arrival of an unexpected ally.

Shortly afterwards the servant reappeared at the door, introducing, with a manifest effort at pronunciation, Signor Daniel Nabaäm De-Schudmoëken.

He was a man between thirty-five and forty years of age, dressed with the rather exaggerated elegance characteristic of artists. His manner of presenting himself was marked by the ease and candor common to those who have long been accustomed to the curiousity of the public and the applause of the concert-hall.

He bowed slightly to those present, kissed the Countess's hand and, taking a letter from his pocketbook, handed it to her with the most refined grace.

"Ah! ah! Baron Teghetoff!" exclaimed the lady, after reading, "he is a gentleman who has never deserted the field of art. And I am so very indebted to him! He has never forgotten to send the most elite and celebrated talents of Europe to me. . . . Last year it was Thalberg, a few days ago Wanwondegger, and today Signor Nabaäm De-Schudmoëken, pianist to His Majesty the King of Belgium, who I am at this moment honoured to present to my closest friends."

Everyone in the room greeted the artist amiably, offering him those flattering banalities which well-mannered people know so well how to lavish even on strangers when the introductions of a lady intercede for them.

"But where have I seen this fellow?" I was in the meantime thinking. "His face is not new to me."

And instead of questioning and complimenting the artist, I fixed such a scrutinizing gaze on him that, in his turn, he began to look at me with marked attention.

That exchange of glances did not escape the Countess. In the belief that she was interpreting my wishes, she introduced me directly to her protégé, and told him my name and sur-name, not without adding a few biographical details.

"Since you intend to play in Milan, Signor Nabaäm De-Schudmoëken, you should meet a few journalists, and I am delighted that here, in my salon, you have been able to make an alliance that can benefit you."

The artist, reading in my looks a certain concern, blushed slightly; but quickly recover-ing from his embarrassment, he reopened his pocketbook, and, taking out a letter, offered it to me with these words:

"To understand, sir, how much I depend on your friendship and protection, you only need read the few lines written here. Being aware of your fame, I wanted to be commended to your good graces.—The person who has written this and who fully vouches for me is said to be one of your best friends."

I moved apart a little, opened the letter, and, barely disguising my surprise and emo-tion, read the following to myself:

Excellent Sir,

I am in Milan for two days, and plan to have a few of my compositions heard in the foyer of La Scala. Have you forgotten the merry evening we spent together on the evening of the 24th of March, 1845, at the Hotel Bonne Femme in Turin? You had vigorously applauded me, the previous day, at a concert at which twenty people were present. Now, after fifteen years, I beg you to hear me again. The man who is presenting himself in Milan under the exotic name of Daniel Nabaäm De-Schudmoëken, pianist to His Majesty the King of Belgium, was called in other times Bartolomeo Scannagatta[1] of Biella. Please, do not betray me! . . . Instead, come and see me tomorrow at the Hotel Del Marino, at around five in the

---

1 The surname Scannagatta can be translated as "Cat-butcher."

evening. We will dine together, and after coffee, if you have the time and the patience to listen to me, I shall explain the secret of my bizarre pseudonym, and tell you a story full of bitterness and madness. I put my trust in you and sign myself,

  your devoted servant
   BARTOLOMEO SCANNAGATTA.

It was really him! My memory had not deceived me—the tone of the letter and the eloquence of the glances which from time to time the artist directed towards me while I read it obliged me to at once offer him a reassuring word.

Advancing towards him, I extended my hand; he offered me his, and in that loyal grasp a silent compact was entered on between us.

A little later, when he had left the room, the Countess began to speak of him in a most enthusiastic manner.

"Let no one forget that he is my protégé," she repeated to those who were part of her gathering; "when the Baron Teghetoff recommends an artist, they are, without doubt, of superior talent. And then . . . what do you think of his name? Daniel . . . Nabaäm De-Schudmoëken? God only knows if I am pronouncing it correctly!"

"He must be, as a pianist, unsurpassed when it comes to difficult pieces," said one of the bystanders; "this can be understood by the many consonants in his name. . . ."

"And also," suggested another, "by the aspirated k preceded by the diphthong."

"Without a doubt," the Countess replied, "these superior artists who come to us from abroad have impressive, and I might say, almost revealing names. Thalberg![1] What does it remind you of? Can you not perhaps hear, in the solemn and almost patriarchal sound of the name, the majestic, sedate pianist who proceeds confidently over melodic waves, like a mighty ship, already tested by tempests and winds? . . . Liszt! . . . Don't you see, in this name, the lightning and thunderbolts flashing

---

1 Sigismond Thalberg (1812-1971) was a Swiss-born composer and one of the greatest pianists of his day.

from the keys? Does it not seem that an electric current, springing from his nervous fingers, is communicated to the strings of the pianoforte and from there to the nerves of his listeners? . . . Hans von Bülow . . ."

The Countess, in pronouncing this name, opened her lips in such a manner that her first aspiration resembled a yawn. Those nearby yawned in concert, repeating I don't know how many times the name of Häääns. . . . And as I was finding it difficult to keep myself from bursting out in indiscrete mirth, I profited from the incident by taking my leave before the grotesqueness of the conversation provoked a crisis.

The next day, at around five in the evening, I went to the Hotel Del Marino, where the musician was waiting to dine with me.

He had had a table set in a small sitting room adjoining his bedroom.

The table was set for four.

"Do we then have other guests?"

"Trustworthy people," the artist replied smiling; "my father and my nephew."

And a little later, just when the waiter was serving the soup, an old man with a wholesome, intelligent face entered the room, accompanied by a big beardless youth who might have been around eighteen years of age.

The introduction was brisk.

"This is my excellent father, who has come from Biella expressly to attend my concert and complain . . ."

"Enough, enough!" the old man interrupted. "Nothing should be discussed in the presence of the soup—we'll talk after."

While dining, I learned that the pianist's father had for many years been the conductor of the orchestra and organist at the church in Biella; he had composed several symphonies and two masses, one for the dead, and the other *live*, and that to he alone did his son owe his great musical erudition and his skill as a player.

Having finished our meal, we sat down in front of the fireplace. The old man had two bottles of Barbera brought, which were, as he put it, his daily cup of coffee. And after he had emptied his first glass:

"Now," he burst out in a tone of voice in which one could sense both annoyance and kindness, "let's hear what Signor Daniel Rabadàn[1] has to say in his defense!"

The pianist lit a cigar and, turning first to me and then to his father, began in this manner:

"As you can see, this wonderful father of mine cannot forgive me for having changed my name. He claims that I have detracted from the already illustrious Scannagatta name part of the glory which rightfully belongs to it. . . ."

"Absolutely!" the old man interrupted, "and let us not forget the damage that you bring to all the Bartolomeos (your nephew included), who have been waiting for centuries for a man of genius to reflect some ray of light on their vilified name."

---

1 Rabadàn is a word used in northern Italian dialects. According to Francesco Cherubini's *Vocabolario milanese-italiano*, published in 1843, it is "the noise that cat's make at night," thus indicating that it is associated with unpleasant sounds. The carnival in Bellinzona, Switzerland, is also called Rabadàn, linking the word with the noise made during such festivities.

The young Bartolomeo, who up to that moment had not opened his mouth, allowed an exclamation of approval to escape from his lips.

"If you interrupt me at every sentence, I shall never be able to justify myself. . . . Allow me to speak. . . . Even priests, before absolving or beginning an excommunication, wait for the guilty to finish their confession. And it's a confession, or at least a sincere statement about my life as an artist that I find myself obliged to make. You, father, know part of it, but I see that it is necessary to remind you. So have the patience to listen to me, and then, as far as the final verdict is concerned, we will submit it to the judgement of an entirely disinterested party, that is, to our journalist friend."

The old man emptied his second glass and pursed his lips in a sign of the great effort silence cost him.

"I do not recollect which philosopher it was," the pianist continued, "who wrote a book to show the influence that names have upon the destiny of individuals. What is certain is that having a nice name, a genial and sympathetic name, generally brings good luck. I have never understood the predilection of our ancestors for appropriating surnames from animals. Gatti, Orsi, Leoni, Bove, Capponi, Galli, even Pulci, Lumaga, Sanguettola, Mosca, Tenca, Ghezzi, Formica, Volpi, Merli, Allocchi, etc. etc.,[1] constitute the majority of the names of Italian families. . . . Then come, in large numbers, the compound surnames where animals likewise occur, such as Pestagalli, Mangiagalli, Caccialupi, Portalupi, Cacciamosche, Pelegatti, etc. etc.;[2] and finally, leaving aside many others, Scannagatta. There is a statistic here that could furnish a historian, or an archeologist, or maybe even a moral philosopher, with a subject worthy of serious consideration. But, in order not to exhaust your patience, I will simply say that the surname Scannagatta was in a certain sense my first misfortune. I have

1 These are various Italian surnames. Translated into English, the relevant part of the sentence would read as follows: "Cats, Bears, Lions, Oxen, Capons, Roosters, even Fleas, Snails, Bloodworms, Flies, Tench, Crows, Ants, Foxes, Blackbirds, Owls, etc. etc."
2 These names can be translated as: "Rooster-stealers, Rooster-eaters, Wolf-hunters, Wolf-carriers, Fly-cathers, Cat-skinners, etc. etc."

no intention of blaming my excellent father, here present; nor do I harbour a grudge against my good brother-in-law who, dipping me into the baptismal font, was happy to make my bad luck even worse by rewarding me with the first name of Bartolomeo.—It is a fact, however, that at the age of six, when I entered the municipal school, to begin the first lessons in the alphabet, I began to experience the baleful influence of my two names. Whenever the teacher pronounced my name during rollcall, a sort of meowing which seemed like a protest against the butchering of cats was heard from behind the other desks;—and when it came time to recite my first lesson and I was unable to speak, the teacher, throwing the book in my face, shouted: 'Away with you—get away with you; you're always going to be a Bartolomeo!'

"These first humiliations irritated me beyond measure, and hurt my feelings to such an extent that one fine day (you, my father, will not have forgotten it) I came home weeping, and expressed to you my firm resolve never to return to the school again. My determination was so unshakable, that you set yourself to work to finish my education, and taught me with much love and patience the fine art of Music. For ten years I led the life of a hermit, rarely leaving the house and always alone, studying almost incessantly. My first musical successes, obtained in the circle of our relatives and friends in Biella, strengthened my courage, and I was even reconciled to the two fatal names, which had been the origin of my childhood misadventures. The time came to hazard into the wide world. Everyone encouraged me to leave Biella; and you yourself, dear father, were convinced that I was a young prodigy.

"In the spring of the year, full of illusions and hopes, I therefore betook myself to the capital of the realm.[1] My brother-in-law Bartolomeo accompanied me. Ignorant of the ways of the world, we had not taken the trouble to provide ourselves with letters of recommendation. We arrived in Turin with no other provisions than my own talents and the sum of one hundred liras, put together by the family to defray the expenses of my first venture. We called on the

[1] Biella is in the region of Piedmont, the capitol of which is Turin.

artistic director of a theatre, and asked if he would engage me to play a few pieces between the acts of a performance.

"'To whom do I have the honour of speaking?' he asked.

"'My name,' my brother-in-law replied, 'is Bartolomeo Zuffolone[1] of Biella, and this young man is Signor Bartolomeo Scannagatta. . . .'

"'So many Bartolomeos!' the *artiste* interrupted, 'and all from Biella? Enough! I'll think about it . . . consider it . . .'

"At that moment another gentleman entered upon the scene, who was, as we afterwards learned, the proprietor of the theatre. The artistic director was obliged to introduce us to him.

"'Zuffolone! Scannagatta! What strange names,' exclaimed this new character, looking us up and down as if we were two beggars. 'What next! Why, with two names like that on the programme, we'd frighten people away.' And, taking the artistic director with him, he left us standing there.

---

1 Zuffolone can be roughly translated as "Big Whistle."

"Confused and humiliated by this initial reception, we left the theatre and strolled for over an hour under the arcades of the Po,[1] talking and trying to decide what to do. By chance we came across a shop that hired out pianofortes. We went in, under pretext of renting an instrument, and after speaking a bit to the owner of the shop and finding him to be a genial sort of man, asked his advice on the matter of giving a concert.

"'A piano recital!' he exclaimed, raising his eyebrows. 'It wouldn't bring in a cent at present . . . One of the most celebrated pianists in Europe is here and is causing a frenzy in the drawing rooms and musical circles—Turinese society is raving about his extraordinary abilities—and a recital would seem like a challenge and would invite unflattering comparisons . . . so . . . I advise against any such attempt.'

"'And what is this musical prodigy's name?' I asked with a slight tinge of irony, which betrayed the restlessness of my youthful pride.

---

1 The "portici di Po" are the arcades of the Via Po, one of the main streets in Turin which leads from the Piazza Castello to the Piazza Vittorio Veneto, the latter being on the Po River.

"'His name . . . his name is,' the renter of pianos said, his voice swelling, '*monsieur* Etzcy!'

"'Bless you!' my brother-in-law and I exclaimed at once, believing the man had sneezed.

"But, seeing that was not speaking, my brother-in-law repeated: 'So his name is . . .?'

"'But didn't I just tell you? Etzcy! . . .'

"'Your nose is exploding!' my brother-in-law groused—and without another word we left the shop.

"How I succeeded, after much trouble and many sacrifices, in giving my first and only concert in Turin, is not worth the trouble to relate. You yourself witnessed"—(and here the narrator directed his words to me)—"you witnessed the poor turnout, the indifferent and almost hostile behavior of the audience. I have never forgotten and never shall forget how you, almost alone, dared to interrupt my last piece with applause and cries of admiration. The friendly shake of the hand and words of encouragement you spoke to me after the concert were the only recompense I received on that wretched evening; without you I, with my heart of a young artist, would have been overcome by despair.

"We returned to Biella in an exceedingly bad frame of mind. The only newspaper that mentioned my debut was a satirical rag in which the theatre critic apologized to his readers for not having attended the concert due to the distrust that the names Scannagatta and Bartolomeo had inspired in him.

"A family meeting was held. You will remember, dear father, how I combated your fixation on me making another attempt, in Milan. I had already arrived at a firm conviction that with the name of Bartolomeo Scannagatta it would not be possible for me to have any success outside my native Biella.

"Your supplications won me over. You convinced me that our greatest error had been to go to Turin without letters of recommendation, and this time you procured half a dozen for me. I set out alone. The name of Bartolomeo Scannagatta appeared to me to be sufficiently grotesque without taking with me, to add to the absurdity, a Bartolomeo Zuffolone. I foresaw that if my brother-in-law went with me to Milan, someone would greet us with the usual sarcastic remark: 'And what could I possibly do with *two* Bartolomeos?' And my presentiment proved true. If my unfortunate name had alienated me from the attention and patronage of the *dilettanti* of Turin, it served me still worse in Milan.

"When I went to the Conservatory to request a private audition, the distinguished director of the establishment received me with paternal benevolence. He assembled the professors and students in the concert hall, accompanying my presentation with encouraging words; but no sooner had he uttered my name than I noticed that some of the young pupils and even a few of the masters had dispersed in order to conceal their hilarity. What else could one expect? I approached the piano reluctantly—played four or five pieces before a listless and inattentive audience, and on quitting my seat, found that there was no one left in the room, apart from the good-natured director.

"The latter moved towards me, placed his hand on my shoulder and, after having praised the pieces I had played, added: 'My dear boy, there is no doubt that you possess a remarkable talent, but nevertheless I feel bound to warn you that, in the current climate, it will be difficult for you to find a path forward in Milan. When it comes to what is called the *great art*, you have a terrible fault, and that fault lies in the desinence of your name.'

"'Oh! so that's it then?' I exclaimed earnestly. 'It still has to come down to this wretched name of Scannagatta! . . .'

"'We have now reached the point,' continued the *direttore-maestro* in a tone that revealed his anguish, 'that names with an Italian desinence no longer have credit in the public eye.—The mania for all things foreign has got so firm a hold on the people, that I am surprised that a dozen teachers born and raised in our country are still tolerated in the Conservatory. Only the week before last, in this very same room where you have found such an indifferent, even hostile audience, a pianist-composer hailing from the north, incomparably inferior to you in every respect, created a great sensation. But he had the good fortune to be named Sfrrrt."

"At this point two cats which had been playing together on the carpet, flew at a bound up the steps leading to the stage. 'You see!' continued the director, 'these names which make cats run away, work quite different miracles in Milan—journalists, musicians, amateurs, professors, all become bewitched. If the vogue which these names without vowels and swollen with aspirations continues much longer, one will not be able to talk about music and concerts without each time spitting out half a dozen teeth.'

"The esteemed old man had revealed to me the true picture of the situation of art and musicians. I presented letters to two or three journalists, who didn't even bother to mention my concert in their columns—and the day after playing at the Santa Radegonda theatre,[1] before a public for the most part composed of shopkeepers and superannuated ex-clerks, who

1 The Teatro Santa Radegonda was a theatre on the Via Santa Radegonda, near the Duomo, which hosted musical performances. In 1930 it became the Teatro Odeon, and in 1986 was turned into the multiplex cinema complex which is currently called the Space Odeon.

had the kindness to loudly applaud me and cry for an encore after two of my pieces, I had the satisfaction of reading in the last pages of a serious newspaper that a pianist by the name of Scannagatta, after having inserted himself in the interlude of a comedy, had departed from Milan in an omnibus full of people from Biella, who had come expressly to conduct their misunderstood genius back home.

"It was then, that, exasperated and dejected, but still confident in my genius and in my future, I resolved to leave Italy, and seek in some foreign parts the recognition of my talents which my own countrymen had denied me. I signed on as a conductor, with an impresario in Stockholm. For twelve years I plunged myself body and soul into music—adapted, composed, transcribed, directed orchestras, gave lessons in singing and piano, gave concerts, and renouncing my name as I had renounced my country, had printed on my visiting cards the name of Daniel Nabaäm De-Schudmoëken, which today is the cause of so much vexation and anger in my father.

"Anyone who has lived for many years away from his own country is aware that, sooner or later, they will be assailed by that malady called home-sickness, even if they had experienced nothing in their homeland but discouragement and bitterness. I too had this nostalgia for home. I had a longing, a thirst, not only to breathe again my native air, but to have a taste of success in that country, which to me, neglected and rejected, would never cease to present itself as an enchanted garden of the arts.

"Could I, should I, after the misfortunes of the past, have resumed my unlucky name of Bartolomeo Scannagatta, precisely on the day when I returned here to ask my compatriots for the baptism of glory? The facts that I have already narrated will suggest the reply. Certain it is that, as soon as I sniffed the air of Milan, I had every reason to rejoice at the resolution I had taken. What a difference between the reception which today you see given to Daniel Nabaäm De-Schudmoëken, and that already given to the poor Bartolomeo Scannagatta of Biella! The day before yesterday, when I presented myself to one of the most noted of your journalists, he went into an ecstasy of admiration as he stared at my visiting card. Another, upon uttering the name Nabaäm, remained open-mouthed for two minutes with his eyes lost behind their lids.

"Two or three members of the Società del Quartetto,[1] on hearing one of my execrable waltzes, fully laden with dissonances, seemed as if assailed by catalepsy—all the patronesses wanted to see me, to claim for themselves the first fruits of my talent—and for the last two days, in the hall of the Conservatory, there has been a competition between the teachers and students as to who can best pronounce my name. This morning I received a four-page letter from a journalist asking forgiveness for my name being printed without the two dots on the oë, and begs me to attribute this irrev-

---

1 The Società del Quartetto di Milano, or the Quartet Society of Milan, was founded in 1864 by Arrigo Boito and others, and has from then until the present time, aside from a period during the second world war, produced each year one of the most prestigious seasons of chamber concerts in Europe.

erence to the ignorance of the typesetter. In short . . ."

"In short," interrupted the musician's father, "since the world is so foolish, so rascally, and so full of prejudices and nonsense . . ."

"That it should be treated as it deserves—right?" And speaking thus, the musician lovingly took the old man's head in his hands, and impressed a kiss on his brow.

"Away! Away!" responded that good old gentleman, now quite pacified. "Call yourself Rabadam, call yourself Balaäm, call yourself whatever you like in the concert hall—but when the public have applauded you, when the ladies have swooned, and when the critics have puffed out their oh! oh! of admiration, I promise you that I shall spring up in the centre of the hall and shout aloud: 'Know, most illustrious, most kind and idiotic gentlemen, that this person who has played as no one else can play, is Signor Bartolomeo Scannagatta, son and pupil of Girolamo Scannagatta, now present, *quondam* organist of the Biella cathedral . . .'"

"And musician, by God! and teacher such as there are few in this world."

"And then we shall go back to Biella together . . ."

"To make good, beautiful music among those who truly understand it, because they have hearts as well as good taste."

Rubly's Trumpet

EVERY DAY the columns of the newspapers report a suicide for love.

And yet listen to them, those beardless philosophers of skepticism! Question them, those floating phantoms in silks, those mummies plastered in cosmetics, who call themselves the women of the great world!

They say that love is a poetical metaphor, a thing subtle and gentle, a natural attraction between the two sexes.

And meanwhile the children of ignoble plebeians love and perish—a beautiful daughter of the people, full of innocence and sunny youth, quietly and serenely lights the charcoal which sends her to sleep for ever; the report of a pistol announces the last of some passionate artist, of a poor labourer, or of a bold soldier, who leave, written with their blood, the two sacred words: I loved!

Suicide is a great folly, and perhaps . . . a crime; but follies and crimes sometimes represent the unique vital symptoms of a generation. The candid and serene souls who breathe love, have need, in order to hold their faith, that someone shall disappear from this world for having loved too well. Love is the religion of the heart; and it is necessary that it should have its own martyrs.

There was a young player of the trumpet, born—if I am not mistaken—on the coast of Dalmatia, and coming in his youth to live in Venice, where at the age of twenty he held a position in the orchestra of the Fenice theatre.

Paolo Rubly had received from nature one of those striking faces, which, once seen, leave an indelible impression.

I recollect him leaving Venice at the same time as me, in the summer of 1857. He was going to Padua to play at the fiera del Santo[1]; I was going as far as Milan.

When he entered the waiting-room, my eyes, my heart, all my mind was absorbed in him, and in the young lady who leaned on his arm.

Most of the passengers on observing him enter the room, were equally impressed. In all the faces I read an emotion of the greatest sympathy.

"Who are they?" I asked of a Venetian gentleman who had just joined me.

"It's Rubly . . . a musician from La Fenice[2] . . . a great trumpet player; and the poor girl who hangs on his arm is his wife—a bride of three months, who may not even live that many more."

"Is this really true, signore?"

1 This was a fair in honor of St. Anthony of Padua and, at the time of this story, one of the principal events of the city.
2 La Fenice was one of the most famous opera houses in Venice. It was especially active during the carnival season when many great operas premiered or were performed there, including some for which Ghislanzoni wrote the librettos. The theatre was destroyed by fire in 1996, but has since then been rebuilt.

"Take a good look at her, and see that there is no room for doubt. The *subtle evil*[1] has been working there for some time."

While we spoke, the young man with his pale companion took a seat in a corner of the room.

They held hands with ingenuous familiarity, like two children—they spoke to each other with their gazes . . . with smiles, as though the power of speech had not been given to them. But the smiles were brief, and passed away, leaving no trace, or only a trace of sadness.

The railway bell rang warning the passengers to take their seats, and all rushed to the door. I went out with the rest, and, leaving behind me those two sympathetic people who had interested me so much, I went in search of my second-class carriage.

Carelessly I entered one of those compartments where smoking is not allowed, and was already moving to come out, when I encountered the young married couple indicating that they wished to enter.

---

1 "*Mal sottile*," i.e. tuberculosis.

"Isn't smoking allowed in here?" the lady asked languidly.

"No, Maria! And also . . . there is only one traveler here . . . and you can settle in comfortably."

Instead of leaving, I retired to the extremity of the carriage, and the two sat together almost opposite me; and, as if no one were present, the young lady rested her head on her husband's shoulder, he drawing her lovingly towards him, smoothing her brown hair and kissing her pale forehead.

"This will do her good," he said to me; "watch how quickly she falls asleep."

He spoke as though he had known me for some time, as though I, conscious of his trouble, and participating in his grief, would receive comfort from his words.

Shortly afterwards (the train had already left the station, and that singular man had never raised his eyes from his lady) he put his forefinger to his lips, and turning to me with an expression the keenest satisfaction, said, "She sleeps! so we shall reach Padua before we know it—she will not suffer! Look! When she sleeps, her cheeks take on a nice pink colour. . . . Would you believe that her malady is serious?"

I was taken aback by the suddenness of the question, and more so by the intense anxiety with which he awaited my reply.

I endeavoured to reassure him, and made him observe that her respiration during sleep was regular and peaceful.

By way of reply he simply pressed my hand—and remained for a few minutes without uttering a word.

Then, contemplating the poor girl with an ineffable expression, "No! It isn't possible . . ." he said, speaking to himself. "A woman loved as you are, my dear Maria, cannot die." And then turning again towards me: "I believe," he said, "that if this poor girl were to die, either she would, after a few days, take me with her, or I would have the power to bring her back to life!"

These words affected me in the sense of a gloomy prophecy. And now, recalling them, I feel moved by a superstitious terror, for the end of the poor trumpeter was as he had himself that day predicted.

The gentleman, who at the railway station had predicted the fate of the sick woman, had not been mistaken.

That feeble flame, which was poor Maria's soul, was dying out in Padua hour by hour. The fiera del Santo having come to a close, the sick woman expressed the desire to be transferred to a small village in the country, near the Euganean hills, where, she hoped, health and strength would be restored to her. One morning a carriage, drawn by a single horse, was seen to leave the city and go in the direction of the pass. Within the carriage, lying on four cushions, was pale Maria smiling sadly at her husband, who sat opposite her, and attended upon her with the gentleness of a mother.

They arrived at the village at sunset. From the verdant hills blew the warm breath of life—on every side a chirping, a jubilation, a festival. The peasants came out of their houses, and seeing the conveyance pass, quieted their song and looked on in astonishment.

The carriage stopped in front of a newly-built house, which was as white as a bride.

Rubly descended to the ground:

"Ah! Then we have arrived! Thank you . . . Paolo . . . how good it is here. Oh . . . here . . . one couldn't die"

"You shall see . . . you shall see the nice little room that I've prepared for you. No . . . don't move, Maria! . . . Wait for the door to be opened . . . and then . . . There, they've opened it. Now come! . . ."

Speaking thus, Rubly took her in his arms, and she abandoned herself to him like a sleeping child—and thus they entered the house and ascended to the upper storey.

"May God restore her health!" exclaimed a young woman, making the sign of the cross. The children who had assembled joyously on the arrival of the carriage, suddenly fell silent.

An old priest shook his head, murmuring, "It would be best if I did not go far away."

Rubly in the meantime had entered the room upstairs and laid down the frail creature who had not yet spoken on a little white bed. "Here you will be well," he said. "Here you will live happily, Maria! Tomorrow morning the birds will come to wake you up like on the day . . . do you remember?—It was in a small room just like this that we woke up on the day after our wedding. . . . You opened the windows at dawn and exclaimed: 'How happy the world is!'"

Maria opened her eyes—she put her hand to Paolo's forehead and, stroking his hair, said: "It's time for you to take a rest. You haven't slept for two nights—go!—tomorrow morning it will be you who opens the windows; it will be you who lets in the beautiful light of dawn. . . . You will see how beautiful I shall be . . . how happy I shall be tomorrow!"

Consumption has an infallible presage of death—joy. When poor Rubly entered the room next day, he opened the window to admit the light, and called softly the name of his Maria, but received no reply. He called a second time, stooping to kiss her, but his lips felt in that kiss the chill of death. Through the window the sounds joyous nature came in, the light of morning poured into the room, and the world appeared still happy, but night and despair had entered into Rubly's soul.

In Padua and Venice it was said for some time that the trumpet-player of La Fenice theatre had lost his reason. Others said that he had committed suicide at his wife's grave. Certain it is that after the death of Maria, Rubly had disappeared from the village where the painful catastrophe had occurred; no one had had any news of him, therefore there was no one who could give news of him to another.

As carnival time drew near, the manager of La Fenice was just about to engage another trumpet player to take the place of the one who had so mysteriously disappeared and had given no sign of his existence; but now a letter comes from Rubly announcing his return to Venice, and promising that he will be present at the first orchestra rehearsal.

At the appointed time Rubly entered the theatre, and seated himself in front of his music stand without saying a word to his colleagues. His noble face, imprinted with a serene melancholy, irresistibly attracted their glances. None dared to break in upon that mysterious silence which seemed to reveal a profound grief and a sublime hope.

But what surprised and struck with great wonder all the members of the orchestra, was the first blast that Rubly evoked from his instrument—a blast that was strong, feverish, but also full of sweetness.

The rehearsal was suspended for a moment. All the members of the orchestra stood up as one and stared at the artist.

Rubly understood his triumph and, without rising from his stool, saluted his colleagues with a look beaming with joy; then as if speaking to himself: "Still not good enough," he murmured softly, "but four or five months of constant practice will make me omnipotent."

During that carnival Rubly's trumpet became famous in Venice, and the frequenters of La Fenice at every new representation noted that the artist progressed significantly. Ladies of delicate temperament, at the flourish of that instrument, grew pale—men of passionate character felt themselves full of an inexplicable sadness, and sometimes they felt forced to flee from the theatre, as one flees instinctively from that which fascinates and subjugates.

In the lanes, Rubly was pointed out as an oddity of the human species. He always walked alone: his gaze, from being fixed on the sky, rapidly would move to the earth, changing expression every moment. Most considered him insane.

That year an exceptionally grand spectacle was to be staged at the theatre in Padua for the fiera del Santo. The season was to open with the opera *Roberto il Diavolo*, directed by Angelo Mariani.[1]

Rubly was called upon to play in the orchestra.

Everyone remembers the fantastic evocation of Beltrame in the convent of Santa Rosalie; everyone knows how in that stupendous and fantastic inspiration the call of the trumpet predominates. Rubly, in performing the potent passages of the sublime master, became himself sublime. Those who were at the

1 *Robert le diable* (Robert the Devil) was an opera composed by Giacomo Meyerbeer, to a libretto written by Eugène Scribe and Germain Delavigne. It was first performed in Paris in 1831. An Italian version was created in 1835 by A. C. di Siena and the opera was performed at the La Fenice in Venice in 1845. Angelo Mariani (1821-1873) was an Italian opera conductor, composer and a friend and collaborator of Verdi, which makes it all but certain that Ghislanzoni knew him personally.

rehearsal, on hearing those accents, felt a chill of terror run through their veins.

The conductor grew pale—he did not remember having ever heard such powerful playing; it seemed to him that the notes of the trumpet represented something supernatural, something divine. And so great was everyone's astonishment and fear that, at the end of the piece, no one rose to applaud, and Mariani, in the profound silence of the theatre, turned to Rubly: "When God needs a trumpet to summon the dead from their graves and call them to the final judgement, He can do no better than to entrust the solemn mission to you—you are predestined to be the archangel of the universal judgement."

At these words there arose from the orchestra and stage a cry of approval.—Rubly did not move from his place. He simply stared on the conductor with a look of doubt and of hope.—He then lowered his head, and clutching the instrument to his breast with the effusion of a friend embracing a friend, said with a sigh: "For the two of us, the moment has now come!"

The next day the musicians from the theatre gathered together for the second rehearsal—but Ruby did not appear. The conductor of the orchestra was presented with a letter, saying, "Forgive me for being unable to keep my commitment today; I have been called away on a matter of great importance—if I do not return within twenty-four hours, do not expect to ever see me again." Is it necessary to add that the letter bore the Rubly's signature? . . .

And you have already divined, O reader, the direction which the poor trumpet-player had taken.—Do not call him mad,—this word represents the nefarious calumny with which the skeptical world pretends to demolish all the great and generous passions. Rubly was controlled by the exaltation of love.

He arrived at the little village in the evening—devotedly he visited the room where his Maria had died; then he went and wandered alone among the fields, until the sounds of human voices from the villas and hills could no longer be heard.—His face, and the manner in which he walked, presented nothing unusual.

He was calm, serene. He carried his trumpet under his arm, wrapped in a green cloth.

Before the hour of midnight had struck he directed his steps towards the little cemetery at the foot of the hill.

The little white village, illuminated by the moon, was silent. The living slept like the dead—the houses were no more animated than the graves.

He approached the low wall—looked around—and then quickly climbed over it. Crosses were scarce in this last resting place of the poor—but there was one, newer that the others, and bordered by flowers. Rubly moved towards it. There, for about a year, his Maria had been lying.

He knelt before the cross, and bending his head, spoke softly, like a young man talking into the ear of his beloved. Indistinct sounds, whispers that were almost imperceptible rose up from the clods of earth.—Perhaps the fervent imagination of the lover believed it heard a familiar voice.

"I have come, Maria! . . . Forgive me if you had to wait. . . . I have suffered as much as you.

But now it is no longer possible for us to live apart—either you are going to come with me or I am never going to leave this place."

Midnight struck.—Rubly rose to his feet and, unwrapping his trumpet, brought it to his lips, and began to emit notes of supernatural witchery. It would be impossible to describe the effects of those sounds, breaking suddenly on the silence of the night, and rebounding with various gradations in the echoes cast through the houses and hills.

Those echoes seemed like the replies of the buried, the wailing of all humanity shaken from a deep and mysterious sleep to the terrors of life.

The village above the cemetery was awoken at the trumpet's first blast—windows lit up— in the light human creatures which had the appearance of shadows could be seen moving about.

Rubly, already strangely effected by the sonorous effects of his trumpet, seemed to recognize in the very real restlessness of the living the miracle of resurrection. The hoopoes and the owls, frightened, flapped their wings and gave forth sinister screeches, adding to the illusion of that fantastic scene. . . .

There was a moment in which the blasts of the trumpet became ghastly. The houses of the living responded with a cry of terror.

It was the final crisis of a sublime delirium. Little by little, the sounds grew softer; the desperation slackened, the notes began to languish and the last one was as limpid and amorous as that of a flute, was like the last spark of a dying fire.

The villagers closed their windows, and went back to their rooms.

The next day, at dawn, the priest and sacristan entered the cemetery, and there found poor Rubly embracing a marble cross. They called out his name, and shook him a little. That noble face was smiling and full of light, but stiffened by death.

The vow of two souls in love had been kept.—Maria had not returned to her Paolo, but he had gone to her.

Autobiography of an Ex-Vocalist

THIRTY-TWO years ago, I was the most handsome lad in Valassina. In the village they called me "Pirletta,"[1] because at the dances there was no one who could defeat me. My father was steward to Count Bavoso,[2] and he could, in such a position, call himself a man of means.

When I was eighteen years of age, the village organist, hearing me sing the litanies, realized that I possessed a tenor voice of great beauty—"one of those voices," he said, "that

---

1 The nickname seems to be derived from the word "piroetta" (pirouette).
2 This name also has a humorous connotation, as "bavoso" means "slobbering" or "drooling". The word as a surname does, however, exist.

might earn between one hundred and two hundred thousand francs a year."

Upon mentioning this discovery to my father, not the slightest emotion was aroused in him; but one day, while I was in the garden planting cabbages and singing to the patches a country air, the Countess Bavoso stopped as she was passing and went into ecstasy upon hearing me.

The Countess was crazy about music, and played the piano in the manner that countesses play. When I had finished planting my cabbages, I heard her call me by name.

"Pirletta," the Countess said to me, "the organist has not deceived me—you really do possess a voice of the rarest quality. . . . All that remains to succeed in the art is that you have access to the other indispensable necessities: Your appearance" (and she regarded me from head to toe through her lorgnette), "is not displeasing to the eye; but I fear that you might not have an ear."

I ingenuously carried my hands to my ears,—the Countess smiled, and, starting off towards the house, invited me to follow her, calling me an imbecile I don't know how many times.

Entering the *gran sala*, Countess Bavoso sat down to the pianoforte. "Let us see," she said, "how high you can sing. . . ."

I did not dare put myself forward. The Countess began to strike the keys of the piano, and after recommending me to open my mouth well, invited me to reproduce with my voice the notes she played.

My ear was perfect, and the Countess was so surprised at my intonation that, turning to the Count, who had entered the room just at the end of the experiment, said: "It would be a shame if such a treasure were lost! You must absolutely let this boy dedicate himself to singing—and we should think about getting him into the Conservatory."

Imagine my surprise, my joy! I related to my father all that had taken place; he shook his head ominously, exclaiming, "So long as they take care of it! . . . So long as I don't have to shell out a cent!" And when, a few days later, he learned that the Count and Countess would take on the responsibility of having me educated at their expense, the good man let it be. But really, he would have preferred if I had remained in the country to oversee the breeding of maggots and the manufacture of little cheeses.

I was at the height of happiness. The idea of going to Milan, all dressed up and cleaned up, playing the fine role of an elegant dandy—the hope of being able, in a few years, to realize a magnificent fortune and, returning to the country, to acquire possessions, build myself a mansion and lead a grand life; all this exalted my spirits to such a degree that I found myself running through the open fields, measuring with my eyes the cultivated land, choosing the places best suited to build my castles—singing, gesticulating throughout the day, anticipating with my eighteen-year-old imagination all the voluptuousness of a golden future.

And I really did have the vocation, the stuff that artists are made of. Suffice it to say that for two years already I had been in love. Among Countess Bavoso's attendants was a brunette by the name of Savina, a witch of beauty and cunning. She had been born in the village, and as children we had played at *gatta cieca*, at *dammelo e prendilo*, at *fuori e dentro*,[1] and other innocent amusements. But after spending a year in Milan in the service of the Countess, she had taken on the airs of a grand lady! When she returned to the villa, in the months of autumn, she looked at everyone with the manner of a sultaness, as if she wanted to say: "Look at these hicks . . . these yokels! . . . Hardly worthy of my notice;" and once, having ventured to offer her a bouquet of carnations, she turned her back upon me, exclaiming: "Take those manure gloves off your hands if you want a lady to accept your flowers!"

But on hearing the news that the Count and Countess Bavoso were sending me to Milan so that I might receive a musical education, Savina's manner towards me suddenly changed. One morning, while everyone was sleeping, and I had come down to the garden to fantasize about my brilliant future, that witch came towards me, all beautiful and smiling, to congratulate me on my good fortune.

---

1 The games mentioned translate as: "blind cat," "give and take," and "outside and inside."

"I hope we shall meet in Milan," she said, ransacking my soul with her thieving pupils. "Naturally, you will call on the Countess . . . and then . . . Milan is huge. The main thing is that when you become an important man, you still deign to talk to us . . . low ones . . . servants . . ."

I felt a terrible desire to throw my arms around her and reassure her of my love and eternal fidelity. I didn't dare much during that first interview; but the sympathetic glances and assurances that I received from that cunning girl brought me to the height of exaltation.

In the village everyone began to treat me with respect and admiration. The organist kept saying that in ten years I would come back a millionaire. I promised him that should his predictions be fulfilled, I would have a new organ built at my expense for the parish church.

For many years there had been stirrings in the town and church councils over the project of having a new and grand bell tower erected; but this vast plan had yet to be put into effect since the municipality and the church council had been so far unable to gather together the necessary funds. The mayor, an open-minded man, having ascertained my views on the subject, proposed to the council that they should defer taking any measures until I was able to contribute funds. The councilors, not having anything better to suggest, realized that the mayor was absolutely correct, and voted unanimously the following as the order of the day:—

> We the undersigned:
>
> Considering that the treasuries of the municipality and the church council are at present empty, we have determined to postpone for ten years the erection of the great bell tower, already planned and discussed, in the confidence that by this time our illustrious and praiseworthy fellow citizen, who presently shows himself to be actuated by the best intentions in this regard, will be able to gather together and furnish the sum required for

the completion of this grandiose
monument which shall be worthy
in every way of our admiration
and that of posterity.

The news of this deliberation excited much
discussion among the villagers. Most, believing the assurances of the organist and the other
authoritive personages were persuaded that
in ten years their wishes would be granted.
Others, however, read the notice with a signif-
icant shake of the head. "Oh! let's wait and see
then," they said, "if he . . . that fellow . . . that
Pirletta . . . can manage to come up with the
money for the bell tower!"

On the first of November I set out for
Milan. My equipment was complete. Count
Bavoso dispensed his used clothes to me,
which, after the village tailor had adjusted
them to my figure, made me quite a marvel.
I embraced my father with tears in my eyes. I
politely took my leave of the curate, the may-
or, and all the local authorities, and amidst
the cheers of the villagers climbed on to the
back of the Countess's carriage. Imagine my

joy when Savina was placed by my side, and I knew that during the eight hours' journey I could have the most intimate conversations with her imaginable!

I need not describe my emotions during that journey. Savina gave me so many proofs of her affection that I promised to marry her as soon as I had completed my musical education.

The day after our arrival in Milan, the Countess began to put forward her efforts to get me into the Conservatory. That woman got what she wished for, and I was admitted without any difficulty. My first master was a man in his fifties, who had a reputation for being incomparable in the art of *formare le voci*.[1]

"Come here, my fine fellow," said he, as he sat down at the piano. "Your noble patroness wants me to believe that you possess a voice of great beauty. Probably madame Countess means to say that your organ does not possess any cardinal defects. Beautiful voices do not come about naturally; I would go so far as saying that voices do not exist in nature. Sounds are works of art; and art, my son, is the fruit of

1 Literally "forming voices," i.e. voice-building lessons.

study and well-regulated practice. In any case, let's see your compass."

The *maestro* touched the pianoforte, and told me to sing with all my strength.

My voice rang out from low C to high B flat with admirable facility. The experiment having terminated, the teacher asked me a strange question:

"Well? What do you intend to do? Do you wish to sing tenor, baritone, or *basso profondo*?"

"To tell you the truth, *signor maestro*, the village organist and the illustrious lady Countess Bavoso have given me to hope that if I sing tenor, in a few years I'll be a millionaire or thereabouts. I promised the mayor that I would contribute ten thousand francs to the erection of the new bell tower. . . ."

"Good heavens!—you have rather lofty ideas, my son!—but, since the Countess wants a tenor, we'll give her what she needs."

The teacher preserved the greatest seriousness while speaking, but perhaps in the depths of his heart he was mocking me.

What a strange thing! this authoritative and celebrated professor who had the pretense to create voices according to the desires of his pupils was, in fact, without one himself.

"A tenor," said he, "with the music that is written for him, should at least be able to do a B natural, a C, and even a C sharp. It follows, therefore, my son, that our design should be to procure these essential notes. The only way to conquer the high notes, is to strengthen the low notes, which are the foundation of the harmonic edifice. Do you imagine it possible that a five or six storey house can be built without first laying massive foundations?"

With this logic of a master builder, the professor set me to practice daily my four lowest notes.

Do re mi fa, fa re mi do—such was the compulsory vocalization of my first exercises. In about three months I lost the B flat; in six months the high A completely disappeared; at the end of the year, from tenor I had become a baritone.

There is no need for me to refrain from saying that my teacher was somewhat preoccupied by my progress. His lessons normally lasted ten minutes, and always closed with his usual expression of dismissal: *"Bravo! molto bene! benissimo!"*

The lessons of the female students lasted longer.

I noticed that all the professors at the Conservatory took special care when it came to the education of the girls. When my teacher inculcated those future queens of the stage in solfeggio, he posed like one inspired, showing the whites of his eyes.—Those lessons were rather tiring for him. But, in the end, most of those girls also lost the faults in their voices, and other things.

At the end of the year my high G threatened to become extinct, and my teacher, noticing this, reported the matter to the director of the school, who put me before the board of professors, who in turn came to the conclusion that I was altogether unfit to continue my studies.

Imagine my surprise, my disappointment, my despair!

I betook myself to Countess Bavoso. The mayor of my village, having come to Milan to attend to certain business matters, was at that moment calling on the Countess. Trembling like a guilty man who appears before a judge, I presented myself—the mayor's presence doubling my anguish.

"*Bravo! molto bene! benissimo!*" commenced the Countess. "What a great honour you do us! Here is a letter from your teacher—read it if you wish to. . . . And then . . . if you still have the courage to appear before us!"

I read, and was exceedingly surprised at the strange things written about me on that piece of paper. I was accused with having neglected my lessons, the progressive and illogical failing of my voice was attributed to some strange vice, to some organic disorder produced by debauchery or other even graver abuses.

I was filled with indignation. "Madame Countess!" I cried out excitedly. "I am surprised that these gentlemen can spread such falsehoods. I have never been absent from a lesson, and my conduct has always been that of an honest fellow . . . The teacher pretended to train my voice for a tenor by commencing to strengthen the lower notes—I followed his advice, and while labouring to consolidate the foundations of the edifice the roof caved in.

That voice-manufacturing professor doesn't have a breath in his body—and yet, when I entered the Conservatory, I had enough breath to blow them all away. . . . In short——"

"In short!" interrupted the Countess. "In short you have disgraced yourself, and must return to the country to hoe turnips! One doesn't lose a B flat and an A natural without some disorientation of the organism caused by orgies and vices.—I know what I am talking about . . . and also things you are unaware of. . . . The mayor here shall bring the news to your father . . . and you yourself shall depart whenever you find it convenient."

Having said this, the Countess gave me a sign of dismissal. The mayor, to reinforce her command, annihilated me with a merciless remark: "What a beautiful bell tower we shall have . . . in the village!"

Crossing the ante-chamber, I felt a tenacious hand grab the arm of my overcoat.

I turned around—it was Savina.

"I heard everything. . . . What is this "flat"[1] that you've lost? I wish to know. . . ."

---

1 In Italian "*bemolle*." "B flat" is "*si bemolle.*"

"Let me be . . . Savina. . . ."

"No! . . . I wish to know. . . . God only knows how many you've done!"

"Savina . . . I'll tell you! . . ."

"Someone's coming . . . you should leave. I'll see you on Sunday . . . at the time of the mass."

I departed from Bavoso's house with my soul in a tempest.

After wandering around the streets of Milan, contemplating various plans, I entered a café where some artists and singing students known to me would often gather. Noticing that I was upset, they questioned me. I told them what had happened.

"Another Maccabeus!"[1] a gentleman of mature age who had been listening to my story exclaimed with biblical bitterness—then, looking squarely at me: "I know Countess Bavoso," he said; "she is a pianist of great talent and a woman of heart—it's a pity she's so much under the sway of the Conservatory!—

---

1 The reference is to Judas Maccabeus, or Judah Maccabee, who led the Maccabean Revolt against the Seleucid Empire in 167 BC.

but still, I have not given up hope of converting her. . . . Who knows!—Would you be willing, my dear fellow, to give me the means for a final attempt?"

My situation was such that the words of that man, however enigmatic, opened my heart to hope.

"If you have but the thread of a voice," continued he, "to which ten or twelve notes might be re-knotted, I will undertake to restore to you in six months that which the Brahmins of the Conservatory took a year to rob you of."

Having said this, he handed me his visiting card, and made me promise to call on him on the following day at ten o'clock in the morning. Imagine my joy, when one of the bystanders, a certain Zilgo, an unengaged tenor, informed me that my patron was the most famous singing teacher in Italy, and in the universe, the only one who really knew how to create a voice or restore it to its original state if it was failing.

The next day I was punctual to my appointment. I was ushered into a large, dimly lit room. The *maestro* was seated at the piano—a dozen pupils of both sexes stood around him in different poses. On my entrance the teacher rose to his feet and, with a Jeramiah-like[1] gesture, pointed me out to those bystanders, chanting the antiphon: "*Venite ad me, vos qui egrotatis; hic salus! Hic vita! Hic bonum!*"[2]

The singing students repeated the psalmody in chorus as I stood staring at them darkly, believing myself to be the victim of some cruel joke.

The teacher advanced towards me, seized me by the hand, and conducted me to the piano.

"As you can see, my dear son, everyone is rejoicing with you. . . . The lost sheep has returned to the good path. . . . Look around you. . . . All these charming and intelligent young ladies and all these gifted and promising young gentlemen, but a few months ago, were, like you, shipwrecked, cast off by the fatal ark of the Conservatory, and abandoned, half dead, to the voracious jaws of the ocean.—I gath-

---

1 Jeremiah, the son of Hilkiah, was one of the major prophets of the Bible.
2 This odd antiphon seems to be of Ghizlanzoni's own invention.

ered these cast aways into my rescue boat; I warmed these dying ones with the flame of real and nonpareil art—divine art! . . . Those who wailed but yesterday, today sing—those who croaked, today trill—the frogs have become nightingales—the cicadas have been transformed into warblers.—So let us leave them in peace.—Let us turn aside from these seekers who are already touching the gates of heaven, to give succour to the latest arrival.— Come here, dear child, and you others gather round.—I wish you all to attend the diagnosis. . . . It is with a corpse that the problems of existence are studied; it is from dying men that we learn the secrets of long life."

The students went away from the piano and seated themselves in a species of amphitheatre that was at the end of the room.

The master began by palpating my head— then carried his hands to the other parts of my body, speaking just so:

"We have here an exceedingly pronounced occiput . . . a nice beginning! . . . Highly developed sensuality . . . procreative strength!—art is but love—one cannot be a true artist, a great artist, without an exceptional susceptibility, or to speak more clearly, excitability of this sympathetic organ. I have told Mademoiselle Guardinaire many times: 'You will become the Cleopatra of singers due to your occiput.'— As far as the parietals are concerned, there is nothing lacking: the frontal zone is in excellent condition! This sturdy percussor of high notes has all the desirable attributes—the ethmoid and sphenoid comply with those of Rubini and Zilgo—wide nostrils, ample canals, adipose thorax, firm clavicle, raised scapula, protruding sacrum—in short, the skeleton of Lablache, of Filippo Galli, and . . . Zilgo. And now we shall see—and this of the highest import—the state of the viscera. . . . Let us first examine the lungs, to see if they function properly and to what degree they still retain their expanding and contracting force."

Having said this, the professor rang a bell and a big housemaid carrying a bellows entered, saying, "Does somebody want to breathe?"

"No," replied the master seriously, "bring the ordnance to test the lungs."

I cannot understand, when I think over it now, how I could have been so foolish as to submit to those zany experiments.—A few moments later the big maid came back in, bearing in her arms a dozen or so volumes. The master ordered me to lay down on a sofa, placed four volumes on my stomach, and in that difficult position made me repeat the ascending and descending scales several times. Mademoiselle Guardinaire, Zilgo the tenor, a rather ugly English girl, and then all the other students passed by me, to study what they called the grand principle of respiration. All appeared surprised at the extraordinary power of my lungs; the maid clapped her hands with delight, exclaiming, "I bet that if I climb on top of him, the C he's letting out from his chest will shoot me right up to the ceiling!"

What I relate undoubtedly seems improbable—yet during that period there were singing teachers in Milan who took chicanery even further.—And do you think this state of affairs is altered at the present day? Ask about the matter of those unfortunate ones who, after having moved to Italy from the frigid north to study the fine art of singing, have returned to their homeland without voice, without money, without profession, without . . . all they had to sacrifice to teachers, theatrical agents, and critics.

After these gymnastic experiments were completed, along with others which I will refrain from mentioning for the sake of brevity, my new teacher gave it as his firm conviction that, following his regime, in less than six months I should regain my beautiful tenor voice, and that in two years, attending well to my studies, I would be able to make a successful debut upon the operatic stage. These assurances sounded quite tempting; but the inspired missionary of art did not seem disposed to give me lessons gratuitously. It was arranged that I should direct a supplication to Countess Bavoso to obtain sufficient money for six months of lessons; the teacher consented to present my letter himself, vocally pleading my cause, and enlarging upon my excellent musical abilities. Everything went well. A week later the Countess summoned me to her residence, and after a long admonition which I listened to with the greatest attention, she made the welcome announcement that she would take it upon herself to pay for my lessons, and that she would furthermore give me a small monthly allowance so that I might live in Milan decently. As a result of this new-found fortune, I was able to renew relations with Savina, who had let me understand that the Countess's coachman had been making her *serious* marriage proposals.

For around two months Signor Minassi[1] (for such was the name of my teacher) trained me in the production of notes, obliging me always, during the lessons, to occupy the awkward and ridiculous position already de-scribed. He, the other students at the school, and the big maid all declared themselves amazed at the extraordinary development of my voice, hour by hour, and minute by min-ute. Mademoiselle Guardinaire, who at the direction of the *maestro* had had two of her teeth pulled, since they had caused her middle

---

1 Author's note: "The anagram of a well-known teacher in Milan, who for many years taught singing by the method herein described."

notes to be a bit dull, advised me to submit to the same operation, assuring me that my voice would derive immense benefit thereby. Zilgo was of the opinion that I should have my tonsils taken out—and the teacher knit his brows, muttering: "We'll see if it's needed—there is always time to correct nature, and I have no doubt that our future Donzelli[1] will sacrifice to art, when art demands it, those superfluities of the organism that might compromise the free flow of the voice."

Unfortunately, the hour of sacrifice was not long to arrive. As a natural result from the violent exercise of respiration, my voice broke on almost every note. All the students were called to counsel—the teacher gave a clear and detailed diagnosis on the pathological nature of the symptoms, which he concluded by declaring that I urgently needed to have my tonsils removed.

At first I made some objections—but all the students *en masse* having opened their mouths and shown me that not a one of them

---

1 Domenico Donzelli (1790-1873) was a celebrated Italian tenor.

had been exempt from the same operation, I allowed myself to follow their example.

The amputation of my tonsils was succeeded by an alarming inflammation—for around twenty days I was not able to emit a note. On returning to the teacher to resume my lessons, to the surprise of all it was found that from baritone I had descended to *basso profondo*.

This discovery created a cataclysm. Minassi extemporized a learned discourse on the revolution of voices, which produced the most lively emotions among the pupils; but Countess Bavoso, having been informed of the metamorphosis which my organ had undergone, informed me by letter that she did not intend to continue to subsidise me, and advised me at the same time to take myself back to the country, where my *basso profondo* voice would be ideal for summoning the cows from the pastures. To that letter, unsealed by the faithless Savina, was added a postscript in bad handwriting, which I quote verbatim thus:

After what happened, you should never again count on my love; this autumn I'll marry Pacicco the coachman.

What was I to do? What could I attempt?—By order of the Countess my father came to Milan, heaped me with reproaches, and insisted that I return with him to the village. On my arrival, about twenty peasants were standing in the piazza awaiting me. Imagine my shame, when a shrill voice cried out from the group: "*In pèe tucc! à l'è scià el campanin!*"[1]

This was the thanks I got from those hicks for the good intentions I had shown by offering to contribute my earnings for the erection of a bell tower!—Indeed, in life's marketplace good intentions have no value.

I no longer wished to leave the house—I made myself invisible. I attended to the work in the garden and the stables, always mute and sullen. My father, fearing that I would fall ill, went to consult the veterinarian.

[1] This is Lombard dialect. The author, in his own footnote, offers a translation into Italian, which we here render: "All hail! the bell tower has come!"

One day the village organist paid me a visit.

"Pirletta," he said, "I cannot be convinced that your beautiful voice has really vanished! Shall we make a trial . . . just for a bit of amusement? . . . I'll have my spinet taken to your bedroom. We can start with the scales—and who knows where they might take us. . . ."[1]

What could one expect? I was not strong enough to overcome the temptation, and with the assistance of the good organist, practiced the solfeggio exercises. My bass voice was by no means a bad one; I studied with moderation, and without violating nature, and learned that which the professors of Milan had disdained to teach me—the fundamental principles of music. I noted my progress, and my heart again opened to hope, and my mind was alight with new dreams.

After two years of regular and tireless study, the organist solemnly informed me that he had nothing more to teach me, and that I had nothing more to learn. "You're ready," he said; "all you have to do now, is get yourself out of the oven and be served."

---

1 A double meaning is here lost in translation, as "*scale*" (scales) in Italian, also means "stairs."

My father furnished me with fifty liras and his blessing, so I could go to Milan in search of a contract. The parish priest, the mayor, the veterinarian, and the excellent organist enlarged my property with a bit of spare change and lots of advice.—I left the village two hours before dawn, and turning towards the fellow who was hitching the cart to the horse, said to him: "I will return in five or six years; and when the bell tower is built, I'll climb to the top and spit on the heads of those jokers who made fun of me."

But in heaven it was not written that I would donate a bell tower to my hometown. I was two years in Milan before getting a contract—and they were two years of hardship, humiliation, and indescribable anguish. Every day I made the round of the theatrical agents who, by way of letter, had continually made me assurances, which always ended with the refrain: "Let us see you!" The next day, however, when I presented myself, they acted as if they could not even see me.

My coat was open at the elbows, and shared its sorrows with my shoes, the soles of which were worn through. I shall not speak of my long fasts, or of nights spent in the open air or on the benches of the Caffé Martini.[1] My friends were a dozen singers of a quenchless availability, who comforted me by affirming that the theatrical agents were a mob of murderers, the public a crowd of imbeciles, and the best paid artists a camorra of schemers without either voice or talent.

Finally (and in that moment, paradise seemed to be opening for me), a theatrical agent invited me by letter to kindly call upon him.—Breathless with joy, I made haste—precipitated myself into his office, and asked with my gaze what my destiny would be.

The agent was a certain Cinguetta, a man of sinister appearance and bad reputation; but at the idea that he intended to offer me a contract, I looked upon him as an angel.

---

1 The Caffé Martini, which opened in 1832 and closed in 1905, was situated near La Scala, and was frequented by writers of the Scapigliatura group, as well as singers, musicians and impresarios. Across the street there was a small park with benches, which might be the benches which Ghislanzoni is referencing.

"Are you disposed," he asked with abrupt kindness, "to do a little twenty-day campaign, singing the part of Zaccaria in *Nabucco*?"[1]

"If it seems . . . if you think . . ."

"It is, as I said, a *little* campaign—so, a good bit of fun, lots of applause, but not much money . . . right? Debutants, as a general rule, are not entitled to compensation and really should, if one wants to strictly obey the law, pay the impresario a fee for the extreme risk they are taking on by putting an artist who is unknown and of doubtful ability on stage. But I have faith in you; I know that you have a beautiful voice and I am also aware of your narrow circumstances. You can see by the present contract how much I have tried to help you—so sign it and tomorrow you shall depart for Arona, where, I have no doubt, you will do honour to my agency."

So speaking, Cinguetta handed me the document which bound me to sing at twenty performances at the theatre of Arona, to be

---

1 *Nabucco* is an opera composed by Giuseppe Verdi to a libretto by Temistocle Solera. Zaccaria, the high priest of the Jews, is a bass role.

there at the opera house in time to attend the harpsichord and orchestra rehearsals, and to provide myself, at my own expense, with the costume necessary for my part. As compensation for my services, the impresario would pay me sixty liras, divided into four installments, according to theatrical practices, leaving to me the responsibility of travelling expenses and the five per cent commission due to the agent.

Naturally I opened my lips to make some objection, but Cinguetta, snatching the paper from my hands, and making as if was going to tear it up, exclaimed with an evil look: "You're all the same! You come by with a thousand requests for a thousand engagements;—a contract is offered to you, and here you are with your grand demands!—My lad . . . let's forget the whole thing. Is all I have to do is tap my heels on the floor and a legion of *bassi profondi* will rise up, ready and willing to sing simply for the love of art!"

There was no point in arguing—with a trembling hand I signed the document, then, terrified of my new situation, folded it up and put it in my coat pocket, and took leave of the theatrical agent, thanking him with my voice, but cursing him in my heart. Cinguetta accompanied me to the door, and as a man suddenly inspired by a brilliant idea:

"By the by," he said, "don't you think it would be best if we settled our accounts at once? This way you would be spared the trouble and expense of sending it by post. . . . The sum you owe me is such a trifle. . . ."

I understood that he was referring to his commission, but I did not have even ten soldi in my pocket and was already beginning to worry about how I would pay for transportation to the opera house. I told Cinguetta frankly what my sad situation was, and explained that, aided by good fortune, I would later on be able to compensate him better still. My words were expressed with the deepest emotion.

"Never mind!" said the agent, with a laugh of hypocritical benevolence. "I love artists and know how to capitalize on their circumstances. . . . If you cannot give me money . . . well . . . I would also be disposed to accept some sort of token of gratitude . . . for example . . . if we look a bit . . ." So saying, he carried his hand to the silver chain that descended from my waistcoat pocket and drew out a little silver watch, the only keepsake I had from my mother, which I had religiously kept to that day despite the most tragic privations. Cinguetta's action was done in such a casual manner, and my resistance was so weak and clumsy, that it was but a moment before the watch had become his prey. In the end I thanked him for accepting, in recognition of the favours he had conferred upon me, such a mean gift.

My debut at the Arona theatre was successful enough, but, in the twenty-five newspapers I was sent from various Italian cities asking for my subscription, I was either not mentioned, or if I was mentioned, it was to refer to me as a dog of the worst species. In any case, the campaign was terminated due to the usual disaster. Halfway through the season the impresario disappeared from the opera house and was nowhere to be found. I lost my last quarter's pay, and was obliged to return to Milan on foot, leaving to the landlord of my lodging as hostage the beard and sandals of the prophet Zaccaria.

For around ten years I was tossed from one theatre to another. The extortions of agents, the blackmail of journalism, the fraud of impresarios, all conspired in keeping my finances at such a very low ebb, that at the end of each season I was never troubled as to what I should do with my surplus. The work I had during carnivals and autumn usually paid the debts of the previous season—and the loss of a quarter's pay, which was already calculated in my budget, kept my appetites in check and imposed on me the most rigid elimination of superfluities. The only regret which still weighs on me is that of having wasted a small part of my pay on appeasing the hunger of four or five theatre critics, who I cannot say if they were greater idiots or rogues. Such weakness was the result of inexperience; but when I got to Florence it fell on me to apply a dozen blows to the snout of a certain Montâsino, a manufacturer of reviews, and I became convinced that there was no better method than this for teaching vulgar journalism the delicacy of style.

At one time I thought that, by a remarkable stroke of luck, I had finally grabbed fortune by the hair. After four long months without work, I was offered a contract for an engagement at the opera house in Lima. The establishment's representative, a personage utterly refulgent with diamonds and other unqualifiable stones, bore the name of Don Diego y Gonzales y Caballero Radamonteros Pordodios de las Quercás.—His name certainly did not lack sonority and the pay he offered to artists was not less resounding. It is enough to say that the emolument he proposed to me, when exchanged into francs, equalled fifty thousand per annum, in addition to two benefit nights, at each of which I would be guaranteed an additional ten thousand.

Before setting sail for the New World, I wrote to the mayor of my village, telling him of my good luck and assuring him at the same time that my intentions regarding the bell tower had not changed in the least.

We embarked at Genoa in a miserable sailing vessel, and after three-months' disastrous navigation, reached our destination. The representative of the opera house had accompanied us to Lima, but the day after our landing, he disappeared. Imagine the confusion and dismay that took place among the opera troop! There were about sixty of us altogether, including singers, musicians, and dancers—and if we squeezed all our pockets, not enough change would have come out to make a *marengo*.[1]

After a week of unutterable anxiety, a certain Arnaldo Sesini, a trader in indiarubber, presented himself at our hotel, and after having condemned the conduct of Don Diego y Gonzales y Caballero Radamonteros Pordodios de las Quercás in the strongest terms, declared himself willing to assume responsibility for the undertaking in his stead and to pay all the artists their first month's wages immediately, as long as they agreed to a new contract, the terms of which were a sixty per cent reduction in salary. We were in no position to make objections. This man Arnaldo Sesini inspired but

---

1 The *marengo* was a gold coin worth twenty francs, minted in Turin after the battle of Marengo (14 June 1800), won by Napoléon Bonaparte against the Austrians. Later the name came to be used in Italy for any one of several coins, including the twenty-franc gold Napoléon, a twenty-franc Swiss coin, and an Italian coin worth twenty liras.

little trust, yet who could we rely on, since Don Diego y Gonzales y Caballero Radamonteros Pordodios de las Quercás had so basely abandoned us? We bowed to necessity; and within a few weeks the theatre of Lima was accordingly opened for operatic performances.

One can bet that of that company of Italian artists very few had the fortune to see their own country again. Many died of yellow fever while travelling to the coasts of the United States. The musicians scattered and performed in cafés and other places of public recreation; the ballerinas and lady choristers who managed to survive the fevers and epidemics, no longer finding worshippers, procured husbands. I drifted through America for twelve years, always intent on economizing my slender wages in order to be able to return to Italy. God only knows how long I should have had to wait to amass the required capital had not the tyranny of homesickness driven me take a gamble . . . like an American.

I went to a large town on the coast in the company of a lady vocalist and a bad pianist. I had posters put up which announced that the celebrated Mario and the unsurpassed Grisi would be giving a concert, singing fifteen pieces which the public would choose. A crowd of those good townsfolk attended, applauded my powerful voice, and went into ecstasies over every trill of my audacious companion; and having harvested a goodly number of dollars, I happily embarked the next day on a merchant ship bound for Genoa.

From my long and disastrous peregrinations, I returned to Italy with only one hundred liras, two parrots, and a monkey.—On re-entering my hotel at Genoa to unpack my baggage, I found that the cage had fallen over,—the two parrots had found themselves free and, taking advantage of their liberty, had flown to parts unknown.

On my arrival at Milan I went to Countess Bavoso's mansion to offer her the monkey as a gift, but learned that she had been dead for some time. Returning to my hometown, I discovered that the mayor, the veterinarian, Savina, the organist,—in fact all, or nearly all, the people that I knew had ceased to exist. My father, dulled by the years, barely recognized me—and when I showed him the little monkey which I held in my arms, he asked me how long I had been married, and if that was my eldest child.

Ten years have now passed since I returned to my native town. I inherited from my father a small cottage and garden, and manage to get by in one way or another, tuning pianos in the houses of gentlemen and singing a few motets in the church. The people in the village all wish me well and do their best to help me, but every time the Town Council meet together to consider the project of erecting a new bell tower, the discussion is cut short with this witticism: *We can wait for the money from Pirletta.*

A PARTIAL LIST OF SNUGGLY BOOKS

www.ingramcontent.com/pod-product-compliance
Ingram Content Group UK Ltd.
Pitfield, Milton Keynes, MK11 3LW, UK
UKHW040807130225
4573UKWH00002B/107

9 781645 251637